The Dove

By Dianne Stewart

Pictures by Jude Daly

Greenwillow Books New York

Pelikan Plaka paints were used for the full-color art.
The text type is ITC Bookman Light.

Printed in Singapore by Tien Wah Press
First Edition   10 9 8 7 6 5 4 3 2 1

Library of Congress Cataloging-in-Publication Data

Stewart, Dianne.
The dove / by Dianne Stewart;
pictures by Jude Daly.
p.   cm.
Summary: A visiting dove provides the answer
to Grandmother Maloko's financial problems
when floodwaters destroy her crops.
ISBN 0-688-11264-1 (trade).
ISBN 0-688-11265-X (lib.)
[1. Floods—Fiction.
2. Grandmothers—Fiction.
3. Pigeons—Fiction.
4. South Africa—Fiction.]
I. Daly, Jude, ill.
II. Title.
PZ7.S84878Do   1993
[E]—dc20   91-45798   CIP   AC

For Rodger, Jessica, Lissa, and Caroline,
Libby and Tony Ardington
—D.S.

For Niki, Jo, and Leo with love
—J.D.

The great flood came to Natal without
warning. Thunder bellowed louder than a herd
of bulls, and heavy rain clouds sent floodwaters racing through the Valley of a Thousand
Hills. The flood took everything it could gather
up in its arms—crops, animals, trees, and
parts of houses. But the house of Lindi and
her grandmother stood firm.

It was spring—planting time—but Grandmother Maloko could not plant her crops until the rain stopped. She spent many rainy days making beaded key rings and necklaces to sell. Without her crops, life would be difficult.

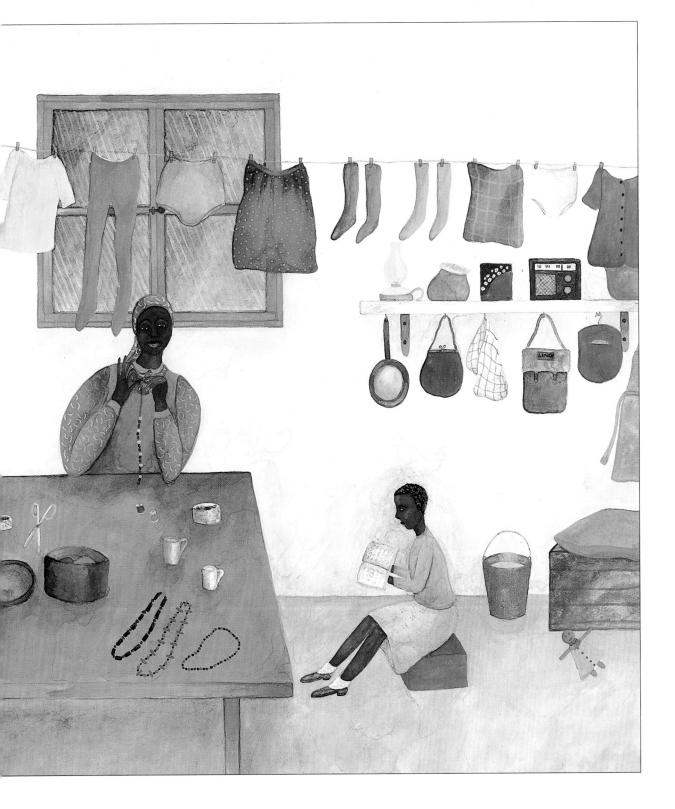

At last the sun forced its way through the cloudy
sky. Lindi and her grandmother hurried outside.
"Nothing is left." Grandmother Maloko sighed,
putting her arm around Lindi.
Just then a dove landed on the ground in front
of them.
"Look," said Grandmother Maloko. "It is like the
dove that Noah sent from the ark to see if the
floodwaters had gone down. Run, Lindi! Get
some food for it."

Lindi scattered the corn and watched the bird
eat. It was hungry. For three days the dove
returned to eat. Then it came no more.

When the land began to dry out, Lindi journeyed with her grandmother to Durban to sell the beadwork. The station was far from their home, and walking was difficult on the muddy, uneven ground.

The train was full. A man offered Grandmother
Maloko a seat, and Lindi stood beside her.
Everyone was talking about the flood, the
damage it had caused, and the many lives,
both human and animal, that had been lost.

When the train arrived in Durban, Grandmother Maloko and Lindi walked through the tourist-filled streets. Between large apartment houses and hotels were small gift shops where Grandmother Maloko hoped to sell her work. None of the shopkeepers bought her wares. "We have too many beaded souvenirs already. You should try to sell them at the beachfront," they said.

At the beachfront Lindi helped Grandmother
Maloko spread out her work. People talked about
the difficult times. Lindi stood watching holiday-
makers enjoying the sea.

Time passed quickly, but by late afternoon they
had sold only one key ring.

"Come, Lindi," said Grandmother Maloko. "It is
late now, and we must go home. Next time we'll
follow the advice of these friends and try the
Community Art Shop in town."

They walked slowly to the station. Grandmother
Maloko looked tired and worried.

Early the next morning Lindi looked out of the
window and thought about the dove. It had been
her friend, and she missed it.
She turned to her grandmother. "Will you help
me make a dove?"
Grandmother Maloko smiled. "Yes, Lindi,
I will help."
They rummaged through the old tin trunk for
material—wire, pins, cotton, and beads.

Grandmother Maloko turned on the radio, and
they sat down together at the table. Lindi cut
the material, and her grandmother threaded
a needle.

"What has one eye and can change the length of
its tail?" asked Grandmother Maloko.

"That's one riddle I can guess," said Lindi. "It's
a needle!"

"You are right." Grandmother Maloko laughed.
First they stuffed the body of the dove, then
they worked on the legs and wings. Finally
they decorated the dove with beads.

"Beautiful!" cried Lindi. "Thank you, thank you.
It is just like the dove that visited us."
Grandmother Maloko put the beads and scraps
away. "It is still too wet to plant the fields." She
sighed. "Tomorrow you must return to school.
I shall go back to Durban to try and sell my
beadwork at the Community Art Shop."
"Could you show them our dove?" asked Lindi
eagerly.
Her grandmother smiled. "Yes, Lindi, I'll take
it with me."

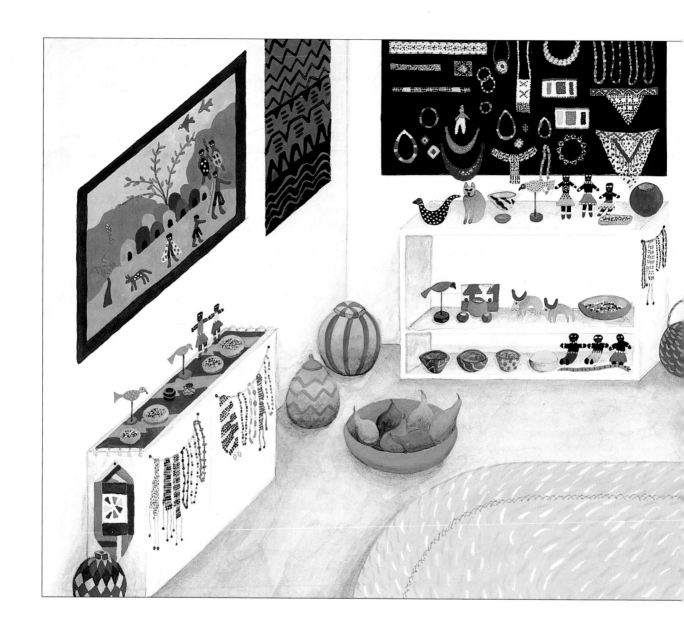

Grandmother Maloko arrived at the Community
Art Shop hot and tired after the long journey.
"I'm sorry," said the saleslady. "We have too many
key rings and necklaces already."

Grandmother Maloko shook her head sadly.
She turned to go, then suddenly remembered
the dove.

She took it carefully out of her bag.
"How unusual," said the saleslady. "It is
beautiful. We have never seen a beaded
bird before. We'll take it."

Grandmother Maloko hurried back
to the station. Now there would be
money for food and fruit for Lindi
until the harvest.

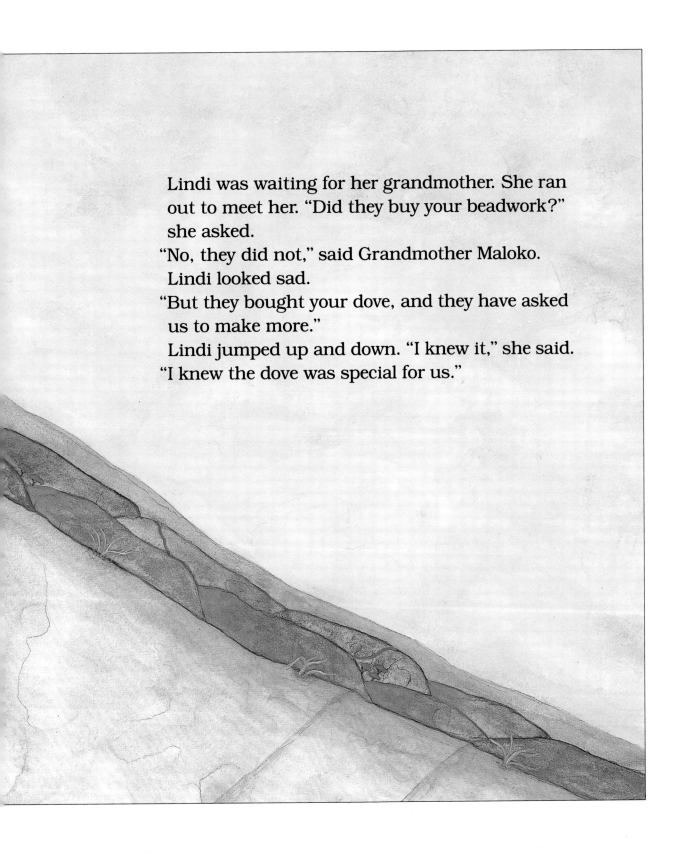

Lindi was waiting for her grandmother. She ran
out to meet her. "Did they buy your beadwork?"
she asked.
"No, they did not," said Grandmother Maloko.
Lindi looked sad.
"But they bought your dove, and they have asked
us to make more."
Lindi jumped up and down. "I knew it," she said.
"I knew the dove was special for us."

During that spring, as the earth came to life,
Grandmother Maloko and Lindi created many
birds, people, and animals from scraps, and
the Community Art Shop bought them all.